That Neighbor Kid

Daniel Miyares

Simon & Schuster Books for Young Readers
NEW YORK LONDON TORONTO SYDNEY NEW DELHI

Hi.

Hi.

For Mom

SIMON & SCHUSTER BOOKS FOR YOUNG READERS

An imprint of Simon & Schuster Children's Publishing Division • 1230 Avenue of the Americas, New York, New York 10020

Copyright © 2017 by Daniel Miyares

All rights reserved, including the right of reproduction in whole or in part in any form.

SIMON & SCHUSTER BOOKS FOR YOUNG READERS is a trademark of Simon & Schuster, Inc.

For information about special discounts for bulk purchases, please contact Simon & Schuster Special Sales at 1-866-506-1949 or business@simonandschuster.com.

The Simon & Schuster Speakers Bureau can bring authors to your live event. For more information or to book an event, contact the Simon & Schuster Speakers Bureau at 1-866-248-3049 or visit our website at www.simonspeakers.com.

The illustrations for this book were rendered in ink and watercolor on Strathmore paper.

Manufactured in China • 0417 SCP • First Edition

2 4 6 8 10 9 7 5 3 1

Library of Congress Cataloging-in-Publication Data

Names: Miyares, Daniel, author, illustrator. • Title: That neighbor kid / Daniel Miyares.

Description: First edition hardcover. | New York : Simon & Schuster Books for Young Readers, [2017] | Summary: In this nearly wordless picture book, a young girl spies on her new neighbor, a young boy who is building something from planks of the fence between their backyards.

Identifiers: LCCN 2016014172 (print) | LCCN 2016044483 (ebook) | ISBN 9781481449793 (hardcover) | ISBN 9781481449809 (ebook)

Subjects: | CYAC: Neighbors—Fiction. | Friendship—Fiction. | Tree houses—Fiction.

Classification: LCC PZ7.M699577 Th 2017

DDC [E]—dc23

LC record available at https://lccn.loc.gov/2016014172